W9-CLN-165

Western District Conference

LOAN LIBRARY

North Newton, Kansas 67117

Call Number
W
E
Sharmat

Accession Number

7843

Date Received 1987

Fund Ed. Com.

DATE DUE

MAY 8 1992		AUG 1 1 2004
MAY 27 1993	AUG 9 1995	MAY 1 8 2005
AUG 1 7 1992	AUG 1 6 1995	OCT 0 2 2006
OCT 1 5 1992	OCT 1 9 199	NOV NOV 1 5 2006
DEC 1 1	MAR 1 8	
APR 2 1 1993	MAY 1 3 97	MAR 2 5 2015
MAY 2 1995	JUN 2 5 99	NO 1 5 '11
JUN 9	AUG 3 0 NOV 1 2014	
SEP 2 1 1993	MAY 3 1 2000 2014	
DEC 2 9 1993	JUL 1 7 1997 2014	
MAY 1 3	JUL 1 2 2000	
OCT 1 1994	NOV NOV	
DEC 2 1994	JUL 2 7 2004	
JUL 2 0 1995		

W.D. LOAN LIBRARY

OEMCO

7843

W
E
Sharmat

Helga High-Up

by Marjorie Weinman Sharmat

pictures by David Neuhaus

SCHOLASTIC
HARDCOVER

SCHOLASTIC INC., NEW YORK

c 1986

unp. illus

Text/copyright © 1987 by Marjorie Weinman Sharmat.
Illustrations copyright © 1987 by David Neuhaus.
All rights reserved. Published by Scholastic Inc.
SCHOLASTIC HARDCOVER is a trademark of Scholastic Inc.
Art direction by Diana Hrisinko
Text design by Sue Ewell

No part of this publication may be reproduced in whole or in part,
or stored in a retrieval system, or transmitted in any form or
by any means, electronic, mechanical, photocopying, recording,
or otherwise, without written permission of the publisher.
For information regarding permission, write to
Scholastic Inc., 730 Broadway, New York, NY 10003.

Library of Congress Cataloging-in-Publication Data
Sharmat, Marjorie Weinman.
Helga High-Up.
Summary: Helga the giraffe finds her incredible
height very useful when she helps capture a robber.
[1. Giraffes—Fiction. 2. Size—Fiction. 3. Animals—
Fiction] I. Neuhaus, David, ill. II. Title.
PZ7.S5299Hg   1987   [E]   86-17752
ISBN 0-590-40692-2

12 11 10 9 8 7 6 5 4 3 2 1   7 8 9/8 0 1 2/9

Printed in the U.S.A.   23

First Scholastic printing, January 1987

Helga High-Up

Helga was tall. Very tall. Taller than anybody.
Everyone called her Helga High-Up.

Helga's mother and father told her they liked looking
up to her.

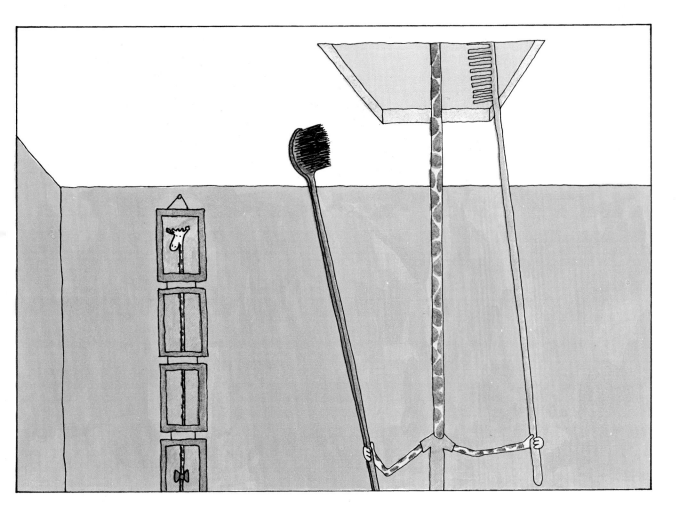

They cut a hole in their ceiling so that Helga had a place for her head.

They bought her special combs and brushes so she could reach up to do her hair.

"Watch out for your head, Helga," they warned when she went through doorways.

But sometimes Helga bumped her head.

And sometimes her ears got squashed.

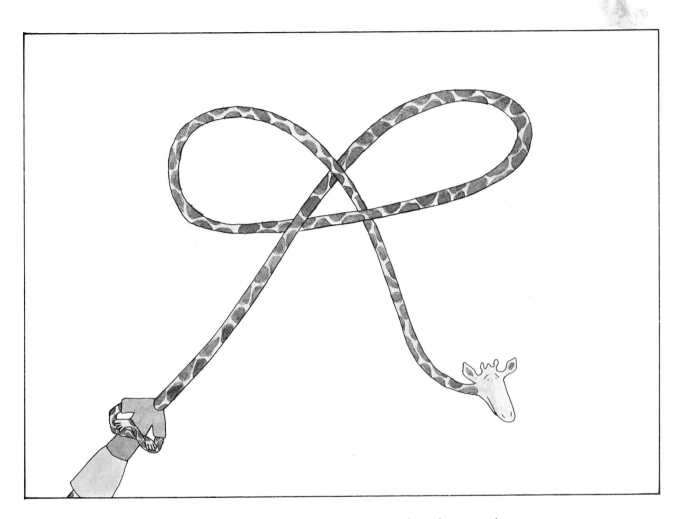

Helga dreamed that she could shrink. But that never
happened in real life. She practiced turning herself
into a pretzel. But that gave her a crick in the neck.

So Helga slumped.

Then her Aunt Minnie said, "Not only is Helga very tall, but she has bad posture, too."

At school Helga had to sit with her head out a window.

At recess, while everyone else pretended to be a robot or a clown, Helga pretended to be a tree.

Everyone thought that Helga didn't want to be friendly.

One day Helga and her classmates went for a walk in the city. "This will be so interesting," said Ms. Rabbit, their teacher.

The walk was more interesting for Helga than her classmates. She saw things that no one else did.

She could see into the windows of buildings from the third to the fifth floors. She kept looking while Ms. Rabbit talked to the class. "Ralston, pay attention. Frances, you, too. Helga, it's not nice to peek. Now come along, class."

Ms. Rabbit and the class turned a corner. Helga went
with them, but stretched her neck backward around the
corner for another look into one fifth floor apartment.

No one heard when Helga gasped, "Oh no!" As she looked into the window of the apartment, she saw a robbery going on. A masked lion had tied up a raccoon and was stealing all her jewelry.

Helga started to walk backward.

"I have to do something," she told herself. "I will stick my head up into the room. That will frighten the robber."

Helga stretched as high as she could. It was the first time in her life that she wished she were even taller.

She stuck her head into the room. "I know it's not nice to peek," she said to the robber, "but I really think you should stop what you're doing."

"Get lost," said the robber.

Helga thought, "I guess I'll just have to go inside that building and get that robber."

Helga bent very, very low to go inside the building. She rushed to the elevator and squeezed herself inside, glad that she had practiced turning herself into a pretzel.

Helga pressed the elevator button. A well-dressed cow tried to crowd into the elevator. "You're a real hog of a giraffe," the cow said, as the door closed.

"I'm on my way to stop a masked lion," Helga said. "That's why I'm presently a pretzel."

"Excuses, excuses," said the cow.

At the fifth floor, Helga untwisted herself as she got out of the elevator.

"YOO HOO!" Helga called down the hallway. "Where is the raccoon being robbed?"

There was no answer.

Helga began running headfirst down the hall. "I'm looking for the raccoon in trouble!"

"You're the one in trouble," roared the masked lion as a door suddenly opened. Helga felt herself being yanked inside an apartment. She hit her head on the top of the door before collapsing on the floor.

"I'm the robber," said the lion.

"I have nothing to steal," Helga said, "unless you want a couple of inches. Or maybe a few feet or yards."

"You're not funny," said the lion. "Go tell your jokes to the raccoon here. I'm leaving."

The lion took his pillowcase full of jewelry and ran.

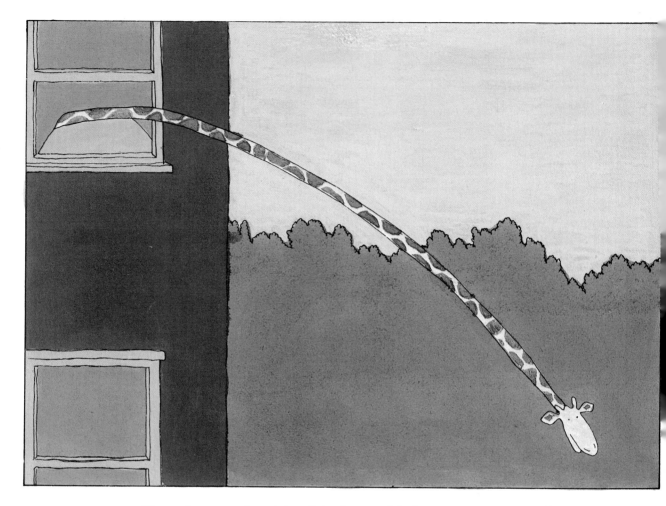

"I can't run after him," Helga told the raccoon. "By the
time I catch the elevator, he'll be gone. But I can follow
him with *this*." She stretched her long neck out the window.
"If I can reach *up*, I can reach *down*."

Down, down went Helga's head and long, long neck
toward the sidewalk, right to where her classmates and
Ms. Rabbit were standing.

"Helga," exclaimed Ms. Rabbit, "we missed you, and we came back to look for you."

Just then the robber ran out of the building.

"Stop him!" yelled Helga. "He's a successful robber."

Ms. Rabbit put out her foot and tripped the lion.
"Not anymore," she said.

Jewelry went flying everywhere.

"Now, class," said Ms. Rabbit, "here is a perfect example of using one's head. Helga knows just how to do it."

"Helga!" the class called. "Come down, come down!"

"I'll be right down," Helga called.

Helga pulled her neck and head inside, and untied the raccoon. She once again became a pretzel and rode the elevator down to the first floor where all of her classmates were waiting for her.

The elevator door opened and everyone cheered!
"Welcome back, Helga the Hero," they said.

"You're great, Helga," said Ralston.

"You're somebody we can all look up to," said
Ms. Rabbit.

All her classmates wanted to walk with Helga. "Tell us about high-up," they said.

"We all want to hear about it," said Ms. Rabbit.

"I didn't think it was such a wonderful place," Helga said. "But now I do. You have to be very tall to find it." Helga stood up straight.

She told everybody about the tops of trees and about clouds and rooftops and all the other interesting things she could see. And do. Like being first to catch the rain, and checking up on birds' nests and finding kites and balloons.

Then she told them how she saw the robbery and what she did about it.

The class cheered again.

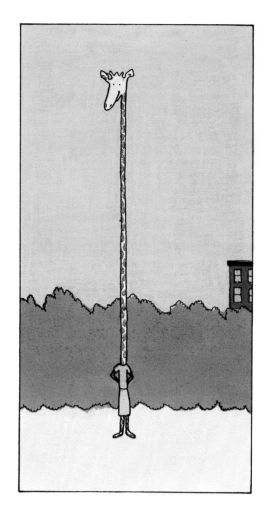

"Helga always uses her head, no matter where it is," said Ms. Rabbit.